# WOODROW
# WILSON

## OUR 28TH PRESIDENT

by Carol Brunelli and Ann Graham Gaines

**The Child's World®**
childsworld.com

1980 Lookout Drive • Mankato, MN 56003-1705
800-599-READ • www.childsworld.com

## ACKNOWLEDGMENTS
**Content Adviser:** David R. Smith, Adjunct Assistant
Professor of History, University of Michigan–Ann Arbor

## PHOTOS
**Cover and page 3:** Bridgeman Images (detail)
**Interior:** Associated Press, 22, 25, 39; Bettmann Archive/Getty
Images, 27; Bridgeman Images, 5; Circa Images/Newscom,
4, 36; Everett Collection/Newscom, 20, 30; Everett Historical/
Shutterstock.com, 10, 37, 38 (left); JT Vintage/ZUMA Press/
Newscom, 19; Library of Congress, Prints and Photographs
Division, 6, 13, 18, 24, 29, 31; Picture History/Newscom, 17;
Woodrow Wilson Presidential Library Photo Collection, Woodrow
Wilson Presidential Library & Museum, Staunton, Virginia, 8, 9,
11, 12, 15, 21, 26, 32, 34, 38 (top right and bottom right)

## COPYRIGHT
Copyright ©2021 by The Child's World®. All rights reserved. No
part of this book may be reproduced or utilized in any form or
by any means without written permission from the publisher.

ISBN 9781503844193 (REINFORCED LIBRARY BINDING)
ISBN 9781503847248 (PORTABLE DOCUMENT FORMAT)
ISBN 9781503848436 (ONLINE MULTI-USER EBOOK)
LCCN 2019958008

Printed in the United States of America

# CONTENTS

*Woodrow Wilson
served as president
from 1913 to 1921.*

CHAPTER ONE

# THE SCHOLAR

At the stroke of midnight on December 28, 1856, Thomas Woodrow Wilson was born to Joseph and Janet Wilson of Staunton, Virginia. Joseph, a Presbyterian minister, and Janet, a daughter of a minister, had met in college in Ohio. After they married, Joseph began preaching in Virginia. Later, the family moved to Georgia, South Carolina, and North Carolina. Joseph and Janet called their first son Tommy. He had two older sisters and one younger brother.

Tommy grew up during difficult times. He was four years old when 11 Southern states left the **Union** to form a new nation. They called it the Confederate States of America. Soon after, the Civil War began. Wilson's earliest memories were of seeing Union soldiers marching into his town. After a battle took place near their home, his mother volunteered to care for wounded Confederate soldiers in a makeshift hospital. In 1865, the war ended when the South became too poor and weak to fight any longer.

*Woodrow Wilson during his college years*

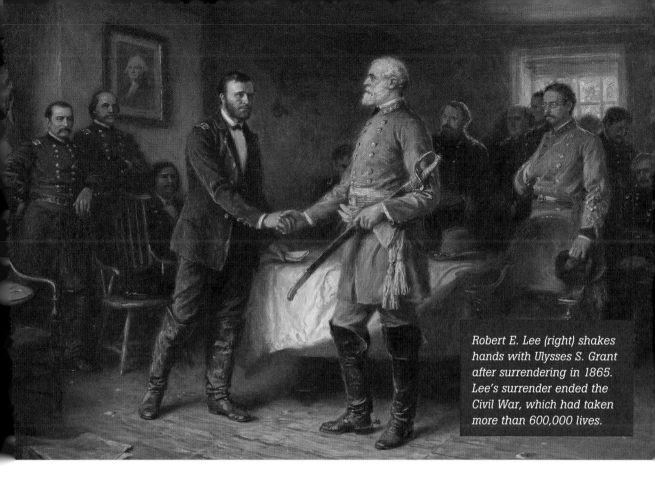

*Robert E. Lee (right) shakes hands with Ulysses S. Grant after surrendering in 1865. Lee's surrender ended the Civil War, which had taken more than 600,000 lives.*

Confederate general Robert E. Lee **surrendered** to Union general Ulysses S. Grant. Tommy never forgot the day he watched Lee pass through his town as a prisoner guarded by Union soldiers.

After the war ended, the **federal** government turned to the task of bringing the Southern states back into the Union. This was a difficult process. The government had to determine whether to punish Confederate leaders. The government also had to settle on how to protect the rights of former slaves. At the same time, the South needed to be rebuilt. Many farms and **plantations** lay in ruins. Tommy saw great misery. Perhaps it was his early memories of war that would make him work so hard for peace later in life, when he was president of the United States.

Many Southern cities and plantations were in ruins following the Civil War (pictured is Richmond, Virginia). Growing up in the South during the postwar years might have given Woodrow Wilson a stronger desire to maintain peace once he became president of the United States. Wilson's father, a prominent minister, also urged his son to make the world a better place.

Tommy's parents tried to make their children's lives happy in spite of the war and its aftermath. Tommy was a smart and talented boy, but he did not do very well in school. In fact, he did not learn the alphabet until he was 9 years old and could not read until about age 12. Although no one knows for certain, he probably suffered from a learning disability. Even though he was not a great student, Tommy had many interests.

He was not very strong, however, and had health problems all of his life. Even so, he played baseball when he could. He also loved to sing and speak in public.

After graduating from high school, Wilson attended Davidson College in Charlotte, North Carolina. By this time, he had grown to almost his full height. He was tall and thin, with piercing eyes. By nature, Wilson was an intense person who fought for his beliefs. Those who did not know him well thought he was always serious, but his friends and family knew that he could sometimes be silly.

At college, Wilson worked hard and earned excellent grades. He especially liked classes that taught him to be a better writer and public speaker. Although Wilson liked Davidson College, he was sick so often that he left after just one year and returned home.

But home was not the same. His parents had moved to Wilmington, North Carolina. Wilson knew no one in Wilmington and spent much of his time studying. He threw himself into learning shorthand, a system that uses symbols and abbreviations to make writing faster. Writing shorthand may have helped him overcome parts of his learning disability. Wilson used shorthand to write his diaries, his class notes, and, later, his presidential speeches.

**Thomas Woodrow Wilson's first memory was of hearing that Abraham Lincoln had been elected president of the United States. He was not quite four years old at the time.**

**Wilson enjoyed playing baseball as a youth and continued to be an avid sports fan throughout his life.**

By 1875, Wilson's health had improved. Instead of returning to Davidson, Wilson went to school at the College of New Jersey in Princeton, New Jersey, which later changed its name to Princeton University. He did well there.

In his heart, Wilson always thought of himself as a Southerner. As a Southerner going to school in New Jersey, he felt lonely and uncomfortable. But the time Wilson spent in Princeton turned out to be meaningful to him. He was surrounded by people who were as smart and thoughtful as he.

Wilson enjoyed many activities at the College of New Jersey. He is shown here, standing third from right, with the Alligator Club, a group of students who dined and relaxed together.

*Wilson returned home frequently during his college years. Here, he is shown sitting at the far left with members of his family and their servants.*

Wilson was excited by the many new ideas he and his classmates talked about every day. Wilson lost his shyness and became the managing editor of the school newspaper, the *Princetonian*. He also studied oratory (the art of giving speeches) and **debate,** skills that would help him later in life.

By the time he graduated in 1879, Wilson had decided to become a lawyer. He entered the University of Virginia Law School. But once again, he became ill and returned to his parents' home.

**Wilson stopped using his first name, Thomas, after he left the University of Virginia.**

Woodrow Wilson never returned to law school. Instead, he studied law on his own for three years. In October 1882, he passed his state's bar examination, a test that allowed him to work as a lawyer. He opened a law office in Atlanta, Georgia. Woodrow had worked as a lawyer for less than a year when he realized he was no longer interested in the law.

Once more, Woodrow went back to school. This time, he enrolled at Johns Hopkins University in Baltimore, Maryland. He hoped to earn a doctoral degree, which is a degree given to people who complete advanced studies at a university. He began studying the American political system and comparing it to that of other countries. To earn his degree, Wilson had to write a long paper called a dissertation. Wilson's dissertation, titled "Congressional Government: A Study in American Politics," was well written and researched. It was later published as a book. In his dissertation, Wilson criticized the American government. He said that Congress was too strong, and that the president was too weak. But by the time he became president, Wilson had changed his mind. He realized that the president of the United States could work to make Congress see his point of view. Presidents often convince members of Congress to introduce and pass **bills.**

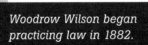

*Woodrow Wilson began practicing law in 1882.*

*While a graduate student at Johns Hopkins University in Baltimore, Woodrow Wilson made time for some extracurricular activities, such as the glee club and debate team. In this photograph from 1883, Wilson (back row, second from left), who sang first tenor, poses with fellow members of the glee club.*

While at Johns Hopkins University, Wilson spent a lot of time at activities outside the classroom. He sang in a **glee club** and was a member of the debate team. He had less time for such things in his last year at school because he married in June 1885. His bride was 25-year-old Ellen Louise Axson.

*Woodrow and Ellen Wilson (seated in chair) had three daughters, Margaret, Eleanor, and Jessie (left to right).*

In September, the couple moved to Pennsylvania. Wilson became a professor at Bryn Mawr College, where he taught classes in government until 1888. Then he accepted a position at Wesleyan University in Connecticut. By that time, he and Ellen had two daughters and would soon have a third. At Wesleyan, Wilson taught history. In his free time, he wrote a textbook, called *The State*, about how different governments worked. His work was highly respected. Woodrow Wilson was making a name for himself.

# ELLEN AXSON WILSON

Woodrow Wilson's first wife, Ellen Axson Wilson, was born in Savannah, Georgia. She and Woodrow had much in common. Both their fathers were Presbyterian ministers, and they had both grown up in the South. One Sunday in 1883, Woodrow saw Ellen while attending her father's church. He liked her immediately. "What a bright and pretty face," he recalled thinking. Never one to waste time, he called on Ellen's father at once, asking to be introduced to the lovely young woman.

Woodrow and Ellen became engaged later that year but delayed their wedding until 1885, when Woodrow was close to finishing his studies at Johns Hopkins University. During this time, Ellen studied painting at the Art Students League in New York City. She loved to paint and continued painting throughout her life.

She was devoted to her husband, whom she called "the greatest man in the world." Wilson loved Ellen equally. "My love for you," he once wrote to her, "released my real personality, and I can never express it perfectly in either act or word away from you."

Ellen Wilson was an important partner for her husband. She edited his writing. She also helped him improve his speeches and learn German. Ellen was always available when Woodrow needed to solve a problem. She gave him advice and encouragement.

# CHAPTER TWO

# ENTRY TO POLITICS

After five years of teaching, Woodrow Wilson was offered a job at his former college, the College of New Jersey (Princeton). It was one of the most renowned colleges in the country. As a professor of government, politics, and public law there, Wilson earned better pay than he had at Wesleyan and became more widely known. He was thrilled with his new life and enjoyed sharing his thoughts on government, society, and education. A few of the university's officials disagreed with some of Wilson's ideas, but students loved him dearly. Each year they voted him their favorite professor.

After 12 years of teaching at Princeton, Wilson became the university's president in 1902. He was now in charge of the university. He hired professors and decided what classes they should teach. As soon as he started this new job, he introduced **reforms,** changes to improve the way the school was run. Wilson borrowed an idea from one of England's finest universities, Oxford. At Oxford, tutors were available to help students learn. Wilson hired tutors to work at Princeton. The students still attended classes, but they also worked one-on-one with the tutors. They could ask questions and make sure they truly understood their lessons. Wilson wanted Princeton to be one of the top universities in the country.

He made sure only the best students were accepted to study there. Even though Wilson wanted only the best for Princeton, he sometimes ran into trouble because of his strong opinions. At times, he had difficulty getting along with other university officials. For example, he wanted to do away with the elite "eating clubs" that some students joined. Instead, he wanted everyone to eat meals together. This idea created an uproar among some university officials, and Wilson had to give in.

*During his years as a Princeton professor, Woodrow Wilson published nine books. They included a biography of George Washington and a five-volume history of the United States.*

**Many important people attended the ceremony where Wilson became the president of Princeton University. The audience included former US president Grover Cleveland, Robert T. Lincoln (son of Abraham Lincoln), educator Booker T. Washington, and author Mark Twain.**

**In 1896, Wilson published a biography of George Washington. It became a best seller.**

Wilson had always dreamed of starting a career in politics. As president of Princeton, he become well known in New Jersey. Then, in 1910, members of the Democratic Party, one of the nation's two major **political parties,** asked Wilson to run for governor of New Jersey. He agreed and won the election easily. Wilson was elected with the backing of influential Democratic politicians and businessmen. But once elected, Wilson earned the respect of common citizens of both political parties.

Wilson belonged to the progressive reform movement. Progressive reformers worked for the rights of ordinary citizens. They thought that average people should have more political power. As governor, Wilson pushed for a law that called for a party's **candidates** for public office to be selected by a vote of the people rather than by a small group of powerful individuals. This change in the law disappointed the businessmen who had helped put him in office. But Wilson wanted to serve everyone to the best of his ability.

*Governor Wilson makes a phone call while at work in his office in New Jersey. Wilson served as governor for just two years before becoming president.*

Woodrow Wilson served as governor for two years. He gained a reputation as a reformer, someone who tries to improve the way the government works. Wilson had many successes in his brief time as governor. His most famous was a workers' compensation law. This law provided payments to the families of workers injured or killed on the job.

Laws like this forced factories and businesses to make their workplaces safer for workers. Many Democratic leaders in other states also wanted to enact worker safety laws. Wilson was invited to speak about his new ideas all across the country. Many people began to see him as national leader in progressive reform.

**Wilson spent more than 30 years at colleges and universities, first as a student, then as a professor, and finally as the president of Princeton University.**

*Wilson traveled by train while running for president in the election of 1912. He gave a speech from the back of the train at each stop.*

By 1911, he had gained the respect of Congressman William Jennings Bryan, a leader in the Democratic Party. Thanks to Bryan's efforts, Wilson received the Democratic Party's presidential **nomination** in 1912. Soon after, he began his **campaign.** He had two opponents, and both had already served as president.

The Republican Party candidate, William Howard Taft, had been elected in 1908. He was running for reelection. Another Republican, Theodore Roosevelt, had been president prior to Taft. Roosevelt had tried to win the Republican nomination in 1912. When he did not, he and his supporters formed another political party called the Progressive Party. Roosevelt ran for president as the Progressive Party candidate.

Wilson and Roosevelt constantly criticized Taft, and it was soon apparent he would not be reelected. That left Wilson and Roosevelt as the major candidates. They were both reformers, who wanted to make the United States a better place to live. They disagreed on one important issue, however. Roosevelt believed in what he called "New Nationalism." He thought the government should stop businesses from growing so large and powerful that they destroyed competition from smaller businesses. Wilson talked about an idea he called "New Freedom." He did not want the government to control big businesses. Instead, he believed the government should help Americans create small businesses. In November, Wilson won the election.

*Wilson (left) shares a laugh with outgoing president William Howard Taft on March 4, 1913, the day Wilson was sworn in as president. Taft disliked being president and was glad to be going home.*

# THE REFORMER

Newly elected president Woodrow Wilson was a firm believer in progressive ideas. After upsetting old habits and making positive changes at Princeton University and in the state government of New Jersey, Wilson was ready to reform the federal government of the United States.

Wilson had been a lively campaigner for the presidency. For weeks on end, Wilson went on a railroad tour of towns and cities across the country. He wrote his speeches aboard the train. When the train stopped, he would deliver his speeches with a colorful flair.

Once elected, he decided to use the same talent to communicate with members of Congress. He wanted their help in enacting his progressive reforms. The US **Constitution** requires that the president give Congress an update on the "State of the Union." For more than a hundred years, presidents had been doing this in written form. But Wilson instead requested to speak to both houses of Congress together. In his speech, he told Congress clearly what his plans for the nation were. Presidents have made annual "State of the Union" speeches ever since.

*Wilson became president at age 56.*

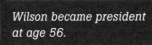

*President Wilson addresses members of Congress on tariff reform in 1913. As a former college professor, Wilson had much experience speaking in front of groups. He was considered a gifted speaker.*

One of Wilson's first goals as president was to lower tariffs, which are taxes on goods brought in from other countries to sell in the United States. Wilson convinced Congress to pass the Underwood Act to lower tariffs. As a result, Americans paid less for goods from overseas.

Wilson had to find a way to replace the money the government lost when it lowered the tariffs. In February 1913, the 16th **Amendment** to the Constitution had taken effect. This amendment allowed the government to tax people's incomes, the money they earned from work and other sources. The government had not yet started collecting the tax, but Wilson decided it was a good way to make up the money lost from the tariffs.

Wilson was a huge sports fan. Here, he throws out the first pitch on the opening day of baseball season in 1916.

Next, Wilson worked to reform banking. He pushed Congress to pass the Federal Reserve Act of 1913. This law gave the government control of interest rates. Interest is money that a bank charges its customers who borrow money. Wilson believed the government should have more control over the banking business. He wanted the government to decide how much interest banks could charge. This would mean that in times of crisis, the government could allow people to pay less interest on the money they borrowed.

For example, if farmers lost all of their crops because of bad weather, they might have to borrow money to pay their bills. With Wilson's new law, the government could decide to charge them low interest.

During his first term in office, Wilson also worked to improve the lives of workers. He signed the Adamson Act into law. This law led to a shorter workday of eight hours for all industrial workers. Another new law made it illegal for factories to hire young children.

At the end of Wilson's first term, Americans were talking about problems in other countries. World War I had begun in Europe in the summer of 1914. Tensions between European nations had been building for a long time. When fighting began, Germany and Austria-Hungary were on one side. Great Britain, France, and Russia were on the other. Woodrow Wilson did not want the United States to join in the war. As president, he worked to convince Americans that the country should remain **neutral.** Most Americans agreed with him, but some sympathized with the British and wanted to help them fight.

**Wilson was the first president to address the nation over the radio.**

**Wilson was the first president to hold press conferences. During his first two years as president, he frequently invited reporters to the White House for question-and-answer sessions.**

**To date, Woodrow Wilson is the only president to hold a doctoral degree.**

People called the conflict the Great War, as all the major powers of Europe were involved. The United States was neutral, so Americans continued to trade goods with many European nations and travel back and forth. Germany developed a powerful underwater vessel called a U-boat. U-boats began attacking British ships. A U-boat attacked a cruise ship named the *Lusitania*. In minutes, the *Lusitania* sank. More than 1,000 innocent passengers were on board, including 128 Americans. President Wilson was outraged. German leaders were regretful. They did not want the United States to enter the war. But other U-boat attacks took more American lives. It was a dismal period in Wilson's presidency, and it would not improve for a long time.

People watch the Lusitania *as it arrives in New York on its maiden voyage in 1907. In 1915, a German U-boat fired a torpedo into the* Lusitania *off the coast of Ireland, killing more than a thousand people, including American citizens. The United States would join the war against Germany two years later.*

Woodrow Wilson proposed to Edith Galt only a few weeks after they met. They were married in December 1915.

As Wilson was dealing with the trouble in Europe, he also faced difficulties in his personal life. His wife, Ellen, had become ill. She was sick for several months before dying on August 6, 1914. The following spring, Wilson met a widow named Edith Galt. They married later that year. Wilson loved Edith deeply. "I have won a sweet companion who will soon make me forget the intolerable loneliness and isolation of the weary months since this terrible war began," he once wrote.

**Wilson was the first president to cross the Atlantic Ocean while in office.**

**Woodrow Wilson and John Tyler were the only two presidents to be widowed and remarry while in office.**

*President Wilson addresses a crowd from the porch of his summer home in New Jersey in 1916. Wilson's campaign for reelection stressed that he had kept the United States out of the Great War.*

In 1916, President Wilson decided to run for another term. His campaign slogan was, "He kept us out of war." Wilson understood that the United States had to prepare for war, but he also wanted it to be ready to make peace. He spoke about his idea for an association of nations. He hoped that the League of Nations, as he planned to call it, would help keep peace in the future.

In the election, Wilson ran against Republican Charles Evans Hughes, a Supreme Court justice. Wilson won the election. His message of peace was what Americans wanted to hear.

# SEGREGATION

Wilson grew up in the South. Like many Southerners of his day, he did not believe that black Americans should have the same rights as white Americans. He supported segregation, a system of laws and practices that kept blacks and whites separated. In fact, Wilson ordered that black government workers be segregated from white workers.

African American leaders criticized Wilson. In November 1914, a group led by civil rights leader William Monroe Trotter met with Wilson at the White House. They explained that African Americans were disappointed in him. They wanted him to stop segregation in the nation's capital and government. The meeting was not productive. Wilson left the meeting, and the group was asked to leave the White House.

Segregation continued to be a problem when the United States entered World War I in 1917. Nearly 400,000 African Americans served in World War I. But black soldiers were treated poorly. Few African Americans received leadership positions. In the army, they served in segregated units that received the worst assignments. The navy assigned black soldiers to food service. The US Marines wouldn't accept them into their ranks

at all. Even so, African Americans fought bravely for their country. Many, such as the solider in this photo, were wounded. The American military remained segregated until 1948, when President Harry Truman issued an order ending the practice.

# CHAPTER FOUR

# A TIME OF WAR

More than anything, Woodrow Wilson wanted peace. His chief desire was to protect the United States from the bloodshed of the Great War. He offered to talk with both sides, hoping to convince them to stop fighting. But Germany stepped up its U-boat attacks on ships. Wilson called the attacks a violation of the long-standing international law known as "the Freedom of the Seas." The idea behind the Freedom of the Seas is that neutral countries can travel and trade freely in the open ocean.

**During World War I, many Americans hated all things German. Phrases with the word *German* were changed. German measles became "liberty measles," and German shepherds were renamed "police dogs." Libraries burned German books, and schools stopped teaching German. Some communities even banned the music of German composers, such as Bach and Beethoven.**

Early in 1917, German U-boats sunk four un-armed American ships. Woodrow Wilson had had enough. On April 2, 1917, Wilson asked Congress to declare war on Germany. He said, "The present German submarine warfare against commerce is a warfare against mankind. It is a war against all nations. We are accepting this challenge. The world must be made safe for **democracy.**"

On April 6, Congress declared war. The war gave Wilson enormous power. He took charge of the United States telegraph and telephone systems. He also launched a major shipbuilding program.

**FOOD WILL WIN THE WAR**
You came here seeking Freedom
You must now help to preserve it
**WHEAT** is needed for the allies
Waste nothing

He put future president Herbert Hoover in charge of the nation's food supplies. Hoover's job was to ensure that Americans had a steady supply of food, even with the disruptions of war. Hoover asked Americans to eat no meat on "Meatless Mondays." He asked them to do without bread and other baked goods on "Wheatless Wednesdays." He encouraged Americans to grow their own vegetables. These efforts were successful.

To pay for the war, Wilson introduced another income tax. It raised about one-third of the $33 billion the American government spent on the war. The government raised more money by selling Liberty **Bonds.** Wilson had the power to **draft** soldiers to increase the size of the military. Of the nearly 5 million American soldiers who served in World War I, more than 2.8 million were draftees. About 50,000 American soldiers were killed in battle during the war.

New army recruits board a train to Camp Upton in New York for basic training in 1917. Overall, about 50,000 American soldiers were killed in combat and over 200,000 were wounded. Thousands of other service members died from disease or accidents during the war.

# THE COMMITTEE ON PUBLIC INFORMATION

At the start of World War I, the American government and its citizens worked to avoid going to war. Wilson had won reelection with the slogan, "He kept us out of war." Peace groups protested against any American involvement. But by 1917, Wilson was certain the United States had to join the fight. He needed to increase support for it among the people.

After Congress declared war in April, President Wilson created the Committee on Public Information. This group, led by a newspaper reporter named George Creel, was formed to convince Americans that going to war was the right thing to do. Creel and the committee handed out millions of pro-war pamphlets to the American people. They hung posters depicting the enemy as a monster and Americans as a brave eagle. Creel organized the "Four-Minute Men." These were people who gave short speeches all over the country in theaters, churches, and other public places. The speeches encouraged men to join the military, explained why the United States was fighting, and criticized the Germans. The Four-Minute Men spoke to millions of people across the nation.

Creel and the Four-Minute Men stirred up feelings against all things German. Unfortunately, this included American citizens whose ancestors came from Germany. German Americans suffered during the war. Sometimes they were threatened or even beaten. To avoid being hurt, some Germans even changed their family names.

THE NAVY NEEDS YOU! DON'T READ AMERICAN HISTORY— MAKE IT!

U·S·NAVY RECRUITING STATION
34 EAST 23rd ST., NEW YORK

*The French held huge parades for Wilson when he arrived in Europe for peace talks in 1919. The sign at the top says* Vive Wilson, *or "Long live Wilson."*

The war was a huge strain on President Wilson. It occupied nearly all of his thoughts and actions. It reached a boiling point in November 1917, when rebels in Russia took over the government and installed a new leader, Vladimir Lenin. Lenin immediately pulled the Russian army out of the war and made a separate peace with Germany. This left Russia's **allies,** Britain and France, feeling defenseless. More than ever, they needed American soldiers and financial support.

On January 8, 1918, Wilson spoke to Congress about his ideas for world peace. That day, he presented what is called his "Fourteen Points" speech.

Each point was an item that Wilson believed must be accomplished to end the war. The final point was to found the League of Nations, an international organization that would work to solve conflicts through negotiation. Wilson believed that this organization could create a new era of world peace. World War I ended in November 1918 when Germany surrendered. Wilson now hoped the League of Nations could become a reality.

The following January, Wilson sailed to Europe to begin peace talks. He met in secret with US allies—Great Britain, France, and Italy. Together they wrote the **Treaty** of Versailles, named after the palace outside of Paris where the talks were held. Among other things, the treaty said that Germany had to pay for all of the damage caused during the war. The treaty also made plans to create the League of Nations.

When Wilson returned home, he had to convince members of the Senate to accept the Treaty of Versailles. His opponents in the Senate did not want the United States to be a part of the League of Nations. To win support from the American people, Wilson toured the nation giving speeches. He said that US leadership in the league was the only way to achieve world peace. He traveled 9,981 miles (16,000 km), giving speeches in 29 cities.

**To conserve fuel during World War I, Wilson began the practice of daylight savings time. By turning clocks ahead one hour in the spring, people didn't need to turn on their lights until later in the evening.**

**Wilson's assistant secretary of the navy was Franklin D. Roosevelt, who became president of the United States in 1933.**

President Wilson (seated in back seat, next to his wife, Edith) greets people during a parade. In 1919, Wilson toured the United States, trying to rally support for the League of Nations. He gave 40 speeches in 22 days.

The effort exhausted him, but still he continued. "We cannot turn back," Wilson told Americans. "We can only go forward, with lifted eyes to follow the vision. America shall in truth show the way."

Finally, on September 25, 1919, while in Pueblo, Colorado, Wilson collapsed. The rest of his trip was canceled, and he returned to Washington, DC. Wilson suffered a serious **stroke** a week later. As a result, the left side of his body was paralyzed, so he could not use one arm and one leg. After his stroke, he also found it difficult to think clearly.

Wilson continued to perform some of his duties as president, but he no longer appeared in public. His cabinet had to help him run the government. When the Senate again rejected the Treaty of Versailles toward the end of Wilson's second term, he was very disappointed.

"I have given my vitality, and almost my life, for the League of Nations," he said. The league was formed and held its first meeting in November, but the United States never joined the organization.

Wilson was too ill to run for reelection in 1920. The Republican candidate, Senator Warren G. Harding, spoke about his dislike of both Woodrow Wilson and the League of Nations. He said the nation needed a "return to normalcy" after the hard times of World War I. Harding easily won the election.

Wilson was rewarded for his peace efforts, however. In December 1920, he won the Nobel Peace Prize. This award is given once a year to the person who has done the most to promote world peace.

Wilson's second term as president ended on March 4, 1921, when Harding entered office. Leaving the White House, Woodrow and Edith Wilson retired to a home on S Street in downtown Washington. Wilson died three years later, on February 3, 1924. In keeping with his wishes, his funeral was small. Still, people lined the streets as the funeral procession went from his home to the National Cathedral, where thousands waited outside to pay their respects. He was buried in a **crypt** in the cathedral, and to this day, he is the only US president buried in Washington, DC.

**Wilson met the airplane carrying the first delivery of the US Airmail Service on May 15, 1918.**

**Wilson's face appears on the $100,000 bill, which is no longer in use.**

**The United Nations headquarters is located in New York City on 18 acres (7.3 hectares) of land along the East River. A wealthy businessman named John D. Rockefeller Jr. donated $8.5 million to help the organization purchase the site.**

**The Woodrow Wilson House on S Street is the only presidential museum in Washington, DC.**

Woodrow Wilson's dream of United States membership to the League of Nations never became a reality. The United States did join an international peacekeeping organization in future years, however. During Franklin Delano Roosevelt's presidency, the US helped found the United Nations, which replaced the League of Nations in 1946. People around the world can thank President Woodrow Wilson for the United Nations, since many of his ideas formed the basis of the organization. Its most important goal is "to save succeeding generations from the scourge of war."

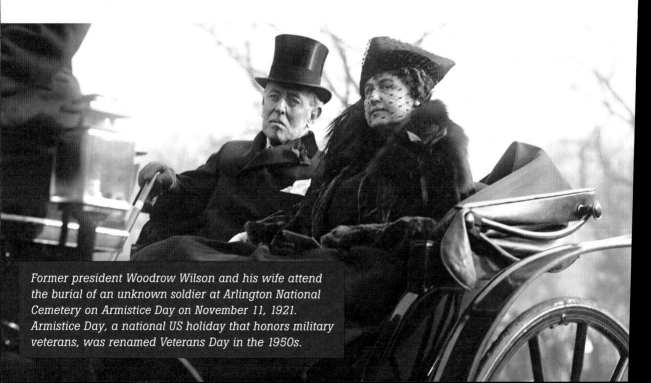

Former president Woodrow Wilson and his wife attend the burial of an unknown soldier at Arlington National Cemetery on Armistice Day on November 11, 1921. Armistice Day, a national US holiday that honors military veterans, was renamed Veterans Day in the 1950s.

# WOODROW WILSON INTERNATIONAL CENTER FOR SCHOLARS

The United States had grown strong early in the 20th century. When Woodrow Wilson felt the United States had no choice but to enter the Great War, he did so as a world leader. When he arrived in Paris for peace talks, parades welcomed him as a hero. In the picture below, he is riding through Paris with French president Raymond Poincaré.

In his design for world peace, Wilson wanted to see all countries, including the United States, give up some of their power and allow the League of Nations to manage relations between nations. He called for free trade among all nations, democratic elections, and agreements that would reduce and control weapons. Some people believe that if Europe and the United States had followed his guidance, World War II could have been prevented.

Whether or not this is true, most historians agree that Woodrow Wilson was America's first "international president." In 1968, Congress decided to honor Wilson's intelligence and desire for world peace and social change by establishing the Woodrow Wilson International Center for Scholars in Washington, DC. At the center, students and researchers from around the world gather to work on projects and share ideas about global affairs, technology, and helping societies in need. Wilson once said, "There is no cause half so sacred as the cause of a people. There is no idea so uplifting as the idea of the service of humanity." These ideas are at the heart of the Woodrow Wilson International Center for Scholars.

# TIME LINE

**1850**   **1870**   **1880**   **1890**   **1900**

**1856**
Thomas Woodrow Wilson is born on December 28 in Staunton, Virginia.

**1873**
Wilson enters Davidson College in Charlotte, North Carolina.

**1875**
Wilson enters the College of New Jersey (later called Princeton University).

**1879**
In June, Wilson graduates from the College of New Jersey. In the fall, he enters the University of Virginia Law School.

**1882**
Wilson passes the Georgia bar examination, which allows him to practice law in that state. He opens an office with a friend from law school.

**1883**
Wilson leaves his law practice. He enrolls at Johns Hopkins University to study for a doctoral degree in history and politics. He meets his future wife, Ellen Axson.

**1885**
Wilson and Ellen Axson marry. He begins working as a professor of history at Bryn Mawr College.

**1886**
Wilson receives a doctoral degree in history and politics from Johns Hopkins University.

**1888**
Wilson accepts a position as a professor of history at Wesleyan University in Middletown, Connecticut.

**1890**
Wilson accepts a position as a professor of law and politics at the College of New Jersey.

**1902**
On October 25, Wilson becomes president of Princeton University.

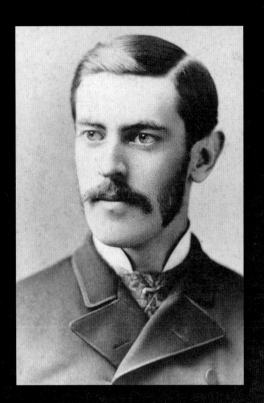

## 1910

### 1910
Wilson is elected governor of New Jersey.

### 1912
Wilson is elected the 28th president of the United States.

### 1913
In February, the 16th Amendment to the Constitution is enacted, allowing the federal government to collect income tax. Wilson is inaugurated on March 4. The Federal Reserve Act passes.

### 1914
Wilson declares that the United States will remain neutral in the war that has started in Europe. Ellen Wilson dies on August 6.

### 1915
On May 7, a German submarine attacks a British ship, the *Lusitania*. Wilson demands that Germany stop attacking nonmilitary ships at sea. On December 18, Wilson marries Edith Galt.

### 1916
Wilson signs an act to make child labor illegal. In November, he is reelected president of the United States.

### 1917
In April, Wilson asks Congress to declare war. Russia withdraws from the war and makes peace with Germany. More than 2.8 million men are drafted into the US armed forces.

### 1918
On January 8, Wilson delivers his Fourteen Points speech to Congress, explaining what he believes must be accomplished to end the war. Germany surrenders in November.

### 1919
Leaders of the Allies meet to work out a peace treaty. In June, the Treaty of Versailles is signed, officially ending World War I. The treaty includes the creation of the League of Nations, which Wilson supports. In September, Wilson suffers a stroke that leaves the left side of his body paralyzed. In November, the Senate rejects the Treaty of Versailles because many senators do not support the League of Nations.

## 1920

### 1920
In November, Warren G. Harding wins the presidential election. Later that month, the League of Nations holds its first meeting. In December, Wilson is awarded the Nobel Peace Prize for his efforts to bring about world peace.

### 1921
Wilson's second term ends when Warren G. Harding enters office. The Wilsons move into a private home in Washington, DC.

### 1924
On February 3, Thomas Woodrow Wilson dies in Washington, DC.

## 1940

### 1946
The League of Nations is replaced by the United Nations (UN), an international organization dedicated to world peace. The United States is among the UN's founding members.

### 1948
The School of Public and International Affairs graduate school at Princeton University is renamed the Woodrow Wilson School of Public and International Affairs.

## 1960

### 1961
Edith Bolling Galt Wilson dies and is buried next to her husband in the National Cathedral.

### 1964
The Woodrow Wilson House is designated a presidential museum.

### 1968
The Woodrow Wilson International Center for Scholars is established.

**allies** (AL-lize): Allies are nations that have agreed to help each other by fighting together against a common enemy. France, Great Britain, and Italy were US allies during World War I.

**amendment** (uh-MEND-munt): An amendment is a change or addition made to the US Constitution or other document. In February 1913, Congress passed the 16th Amendment.

**bills** (BILZ): Bills are ideas for new laws that are presented to a group of lawmakers. After Congress passes a bill, the president either signs it into law or rejects it.

**bonds** (BONDZ): Bonds are certificates that enable the government to raise money. When people buy bonds, they are loaning the government money. The government pays back the money with interest after a certain period of time.

**campaign** (kam-PAYN): A campaign is the process of running for an election, including activities such as giving speeches or attending rallies. Wilson began his first campaign for president in 1912.

**candidates** (KAN-duh-dates): Candidates are people running in an election. Wilson was the Democratic Party's presidential candidate in 1912 and 1916.

**civil rights** (SI-vul RITES): Civil rights are basic rights that are guaranteed to all people under the US Constitution. Civil rights leaders were disappointed in Wilson.

**constitution** (kon-stih-TOO-shun): A constitution is the set of basic principles that govern a state, country, or society. According to the US Constitution, only Congress can declare war.

**crypt** (KRIPT): A crypt is a chamber under the main floor of a church. Wilson is buried in a crypt at the National Cathedral.

**debate** (di-BAYT): A debate is a formal meeting in which people discuss a topic. While at Johns Hopkins, Wilson belonged to a debate team.

**democracy** (di-MAW-kruh-see): A democracy is a nation in which the people control the government by electing their own leaders. The United States is a democracy.

**draft** (DRAFT): When governments draft people into the armed forces, they require them to join. The US government drafted more than 2.8 million men during World War I.

**federal** (FED-er-ul): Federal means having to do with the central government of the United States, rather than a state or city government. Wilson planned to reform the federal government.

**glee club** (GLEE KLUB): A glee club is a group of people who sing songs together. Wilson sang in a glee club while attending Johns Hopkins University.

**neutral** (NOO-trul): If a country is neutral, it does not take sides during a conflict or war. Wilson wanted the United States to remain neutral during World War I.

**nomination** (nom-ih-NAY-shun): If someone receives a nomination, he or she is chosen by a political party to run for an office. Wilson received the Democratic Party's presidential nomination in 1912 and 1916.

**plantations** (plan-TAY-shunz): Plantations are large farms that grow primarily one crop such as tobacco, sugarcane, or cotton. Many Southern plantations were destroyed during the Civil War.

**political parties** (puh-LIT-ih-kul PAR-teez): Political parties are groups of people who share similar ideas about how to run a government. The two major political parties in the United States are the Democratic Party and the Republican Party.

**reforms** (reh-FORMZ): Reforms are changes that improve something. As an educator and a politician, Wilson introduced reforms.

**segregation** (seg-greh-GAY-shun): Segregation is the separation of people by race. Wilson supported segregation.

**stroke** (STROHK): A stroke is a sudden injury to the brain that occurs when a blood vessel breaks or becomes blocked. Wilson suffered a stroke in 1919.

**surrendered** (suh-REN-durd): If an army surrendered, it gave up to its enemy. The Germans surrendered in 1918.

**treaty** (TREE-tee): A treaty is a formal agreement between nations. The Treaty of Versailles ended World War I.

**union** (YOON-yen): A union is the joining together of two people or groups of people, such as states. The Union is another name for the United States.

# THE UNITED STATES GOVERNMENT

The United States government is divided into three equal branches: the executive, the legislative, and the judicial. This division helps prevent abuses of power because each branch has to answer to the other two. No one branch can become too powerful.

## EXECUTIVE BRANCH

President
Vice President
Departments

The job of the executive branch is to enforce the laws. It is headed by the president, who serves as the spokesperson for the United States around the world. The president has the power to sign bills into law. He or she also appoints important officials, such as federal judges, who are then confirmed by the US Senate. The president is also the commander in chief of the US military. He or she is assisted by the vice president, who takes over if the president dies or cannot carry out the duties of the office.

The executive branch also includes various departments, each focused on a specific topic. They include the Defense Department, the Justice Department, and the Agriculture Department. The department heads, along with other officials such as the vice president, serve as the president's closest advisers, called the cabinet.

## LEGISLATIVE BRANCH

Congress: Senate and the
House of Representatives

The job of the legislative branch is to make the laws. It consists of Congress, which is divided into two parts: the Senate and the House of Representatives. The Senate has 100 members, and the House of Representatives has 435 members. Each state has two senators. The number of representatives a state has varies depending on the state's population.

Besides making laws, Congress also passes budgets and enacts taxes. In addition, it is responsible for declaring war, maintaining the military, and regulating trade with other countries.

## JUDICIAL BRANCH

Supreme Court
Courts of Appeals
District Courts

The job of the judicial branch is to interpret the laws. It consists of the nation's federal courts. Trials are held in district courts. During trials, judges must decide what laws mean and how they apply. Courts of appeals review the decisions made in district courts.

The nation's highest court is the Supreme Court. If someone disagrees with a court of appeals ruling, he or she can ask the Supreme Court to review it. The Supreme Court may refuse. The Supreme Court makes sure that decisions and laws do not violate the Constitution.

# CHOOSING THE PRESIDENT

It may seem odd, but American voters don't elect the president directly. Instead, the president is chosen using what is called the Electoral College.

Each state gets as many votes in the Electoral College as its combined total of senators and representatives in Congress. For example, Iowa has two senators and four representatives, so it gets six electoral votes. Although the District of Columbia does not have any voting members in Congress, it gets three electoral votes. Usually, the candidate who wins the most votes in any given state receives all of that state's electoral votes.

To become president, a candidate must get more than half of the Electoral College votes. There are a total of 538 votes in the Electoral College, so a candidate needs 270 votes to win. If nobody receives 270 Electoral College votes, the House of Representatives chooses the president.

With the Electoral College system, the person who receives the most votes nationwide does not always receive the most electoral votes. This happened most recently in 2016, when Hillary Clinton received nearly 2.9 million more national votes than Donald J. Trump. Trump became president because he had more Electoral College votes.

# THE WHITE HOUSE

The White House is the official home of the president of the United States. It is located at 1600 Pennsylvania Avenue NW in Washington, DC. In 1792, a contest was held to select the architect who would design the president's home. James Hoban won. Construction took eight years.

The first president, George Washington, never lived in the White House. The second president, John Adams, moved into the house in 1800, though the inside was not yet complete. During the War of 1812, British soldiers burned down much of the White House. It was rebuilt several years later.

The White House was changed through the years. Porches were added, and President Theodore Roosevelt added the West Wing. President William Taft changed the shape of the presidential office, making it into the famous Oval Office. While Harry Truman was president, the old house was discovered to be structurally weak. All the walls were reinforced with steel, and the rooms were rebuilt.

Today, the White House has 132 rooms (including 35 bathrooms), 28 fireplaces, and 3 elevators. It takes 570 gallons of paint to cover the outside of the six-story building. The White House provides the president with many ways to relax. It includes a putting green, a jogging track, a swimming pool, a basketball and tennis court, and beautifully landscaped gardens. The White House also has a movie theater, a billiard room, and a one-lane bowling alley.

The job of president of the United States is challenging. It is probably one of the most stressful jobs in the world. Because of this, presidents are paid well, though not nearly as well as the leaders of large corporations. In 2020, the president earned $400,000 a year. Presidents also receive extra benefits that make the demanding job a little more appealing.

★ **Camp David:** In the 1940s, President Franklin D. Roosevelt chose this heavily wooded spot in the mountains of Maryland to be the presidential retreat, where presidents can relax. Even though it is a retreat, world business is conducted there. Most famously, President Jimmy Carter met with Middle Eastern leaders at Camp David in 1978. The result was a peace agreement between Israel and Egypt.

★ ***Air Force One:*** The president flies on a jet called *Air Force One*. It is a Boeing 747-200B that has been modified to meet the president's needs. *Air Force One* is the size of a large home. It is equipped with a dining room, sleeping quarters, a conference room, and office space. It also has two kitchens that can provide food for up to 100 people.

★ **The Secret Service:** While not the most glamorous of the president's perks, the Secret Service is one of the most important. The Secret Service is a group of highly trained agents who protect the president and the president's family.

★ **The Presidential State Car:** The presidential state car is a customized Cadillac limousine. It has been armored to protect the president in case of attack. Inside the plush car are a foldaway desk, an entertainment center, and a communications console.

★ **The Food:** The White House has five chefs who will make any food the president wants. The White House also has an extensive wine collection and vegetable and fruit gardens.

★ **Retirement:** A former president receives a pension, or retirement pay, of just under $208,000 a year. Former presidents also receive health care coverage and Secret Service protection for the rest of their lives.

## QUALIFICATIONS

To run for president, a candidate must
- ★ be at least 35 years old
- ★ be a citizen who was born in the United States
- ★ have lived in the United States for 14 years

## TERM OF OFFICE

A president's term of office is four years. No president can stay in office for more than two terms.

## ELECTION DATE

The presidential election takes place every four years on the first Tuesday after November 1.

## INAUGURATION DATE

Presidents are inaugurated on January 20.

## OATH OF OFFICE

I do solemnly swear I will faithfully execute the office of the President of the United States and will to the best of my ability preserve, protect, and defend the Constitution of the United States.

## WRITE A LETTER TO THE PRESIDENT

One of the best things about being a US citizen is that Americans get to participate in their government. They can speak out if they feel government leaders aren't doing their jobs. They can also praise leaders who are going the extra mile. Do you have something you'd like the president to do? Should the president worry more about the environment and the effects of climate change? Should the government spend more money on our schools? You can write a letter to the president to say how you feel!

> 1600 Pennsylvania Avenue NW
> Washington, DC 20500

You can even write a message to the president at **whitehouse.gov/contact**.

# FOR MORE INFORMATION

## BOOKS

Crompton, Samuel Willard. *How Woodrow Wilson Fought World War I.* New York, NY: Enslow, 2017.

Frith, Margaret, and Andrew Thomson (illustrator). *Who Was Woodrow Wilson?* New York, NY: Grosset & Dunlap, 2015.

Orr, Tamra B. *African Americans in the Armed Forces.* New York, NY: Lucent, 2020.

Tinari, Leah. *The Presidents: Portraits of History.* New York, NY: Aladdin, 2019.

Ziff, John. *World War I.* Philadelphia, PA: Mason Crest, 2016.

## INTERNET SITES

Visit our website for lots of links about Woodrow Wilson and other US presidents:

### childsworld.com/links

*Note to Parents, Teachers, and Librarians: We routinely verify our web links to make sure they are safe, active sites. Encourage your readers to check them out!*

# INDEX